HIGH, HOMIES & LETTERS

ANUSHKA BHARTI

Made with ♥ on the Notion Press Platform
www.notionpress.com

To my family who loves me endlessly and has done their best for me.

To the splendid mentors of my alma mater and present institution who have moulded my personality in the present form.

To all my precious friends who have accepted me with my flaws and being the reason for my innumerable laughters,moments and strength.

To all those people and life experiences who have proved to be a lesson and helped me gain better perspectives about various aspects of life.

To the Supreme Power who makes me feel grateful about everything I possess, providing a constant boost to grow and glow.

Contents

Foreword — *vii*

Preface — *ix*

Prologue — *xi*

1. Letter 1: Young Love Which Feels Never-ending... — 1

2. Letter 2 :the Bursted Bubble... — 4

3. Letter 3 :not Better Than Your Ex For Sure... — 7

4. Letter 4 : Love Is... ; Love Isn't... — 9

5. Letter 5 : Together As Bittersweet Homies... — 11

6. Letter 6 : My Homie Has Beautiful Eyes, Nose, Lips And Vibes... — 13

7. Letter 7 :the Burning Passion In My Heart... — 16

8. Letter 8 :the Dreamy Fantasy Of That Lovely Night And Us... — 18

9. Letter 9:the Shadow Of Bright Light... — 20

10. Letter 10 :binding My Overthinking Soul With Your Dose Of Love... — 23

Let The Stars Decide... — 25

Foreword

"Emotions are a powerful and charming form of expression."

In this materialistic, selfish, and egoistic world there should be a person in your life with whom you can share your emotions without any kind of false or pseudo-identity and filters. Someone with whom you can live as you are in REALITY. Apart from parents and relatives, everyone needs a companion, whether that person is a husband/ wife, sibling, cousin or friend. It is something that is not just important in daily life but also plays a beautiful part in this chaotic life.

There are very few people around you who can truly and honestly accept your reality, your LOVE and your CARE. Moreover, if you have that special person in this huge kind of universal mess then, darling ,you are so lucky and it becomes more beautiful when you both start understanding each other's emotions and not just compromise with them. This is something which is from my perspective or view about BONDING and a special person.

I am **Vishal B. Gola**, one of India's beginners and modern mystical authors and a close friend of *Anushka* who is herself an inspiration for me in my writing career. She is a brilliant writer and speaker who can melt anyone's heart with her soulful words and vocabulary. I have read all of her poems and works. She not only writes a text or poem but also represents the inner beauty of any kind of relationship. In her debut book "High, Homies & Letters" she has brilliantly and empathically presented the emotions from the eyes of youngsters for their special person. I think it is very common in the current phase of our time but also so sensitive because **you just can be who you are in front of someone with whom you are in love, so easily**. But to pen down every single drop of the emotions of such a relationship without any filter and even thinking about its future in this selfish world where every other being wants to make you sad, is so difficult. As an author, it is always challenging to write something about UNFILTERED LOVE because every word that an author writes comes out as a trigger along the upcoming turning point for society and the world.

In the end, best wishes to my best friend and her debut book which can reflect on the mindset of several people and shows the real beauty of LOVE.

Preface

The best person I could have ever vibed with.
Thanks for sharing each and every smile, tear, laughter,
yell, sunshine and shadow with me.
You are eternely irreplaceable, valuable and
unforgettable.
I love you, Homie>>>

Prologue

"Everything is fair in love and war"

You would have heard this cliche sentence millions of times in your life, wouldn't you?

I'm sure it would be a **yes**.

Apparently being a peace-loving person, I won't talk of war as of now but love, coming from a hopelessly romantic person as well. This can be something which is just undefined and as complex as the most complicated question in calculus of maths in plus two for a primary school student or as simple as the alphabets for a high school student.

The definition of love for every individual changes according to the experiences one gains with respect to the same.

You might have fallen in love too at some point of time. People literally have varied concepts for this single word. Some get their first love as the right one, being lucky in getting a partner who makes them feel the best. Some get failures in their first love which makes them learn various lessons and refines them into a better and stronger personality. They perceive things and their surroundings in a far mature manner after the failure and have a clearer picture of their priorities. It's them who actually fears the concept of love, nine out of ten times. If at all, they get someone whom they love, it's just out of an unexpected nut and the keeper in them values them the most.

Even after being completely drenched in love with someone, there are various other factors which define their togetherness including trust, level of comfort zone, honesty, mutual respect and most importantly, vibes, above all. Something which affects two people in love after vibes include friendship and that too, on a very important note. You actually cannot love a person if you aren't friends with them. Being friends with that person makes you aware of that individual as a person in a lot of specific ways. The positives and negatives of that person can be explored well in a deeper perspective if you are his/ her best friend. Keeping the bond of your friendship above anything lets you be in a very comfortable zone with that person, so much so that you can be brutally honest with the same in case of any conflicts. You can share yourself in an unfiltered and better manner and that increases the level of emotional intimacy between you both.

> *"Love is imperfectly perfect; one of the rarest cherubic sanctions only a handful of lucky ones are truly blessed with!*
>
> *Love isn't life certainly; but it's one of the most cherished feelings in the world with an unique invincibility to turn your life into a bit more beautiful one.*
>
> *Love is a bittersweet bliss!"*

Do you wish to explore this bittersweet bliss of love from my eyes?

Let's have a glimpse of love reflected in the *letters to my homie.*

ONE

LETTER 1: YOUNG LOVE WHICH FEELS NEVER-ENDING...

The moon screams an unfurled message for you and this room sings our beautiful untold bond. It's just to cover my insane world of chaos I feel even with the thought of losing you. Your breath feels so very mandatory to me. The breeze continuously warns me not to overexpose my vulnerable side but it's just that I can't afford losing a chance to lose myself in you. Your touch seems so soothing without any weak knees. Even though my heart rate shoots up, it's not anxious. It's just a calm vibe flowing all over with my heart pounding as a tiny child. Most of the things seem so easy when you are by my side. I know we can't be intersections in our lives ever together but I'm relieved by the fact that we can be parallel shooting stars walking alongside together though without a union. The dew on the leaves shine unusually when you caress my face with your fingers. I wish for eternal time to stop by literally when you do so . Maybe that could be happening in another parallel world of this universe where you would just be mine altogether and not just a parallel shooting star . Don't ever try to feel that I'm harbouring any negative thoughts by thinking all this....it's just that my expectations really cease to exist when it comes to you; instead there are just hopes. Hopes can or cannot be true and I know this completely and that's the only reason I have hopes about us and not expectations. It's just you for the very first time when I actually feel to live in the moments, cherishing the time which I'm living rather than worrying about the fact if or whether those moments will be forever or not.

All the different emotions are served in my platter of this very new sensation. I had the fear of not being valued and taken for granted which haunted me since I had been treated as such always. The fear of being replaced at any point of time even after being available for people whom I love was so very prominent in my heart that I hesitated to be attached all over again. Most importantly, I'm not telling you all these fears of mine in order to compare you with my past bonds or people as such or to have a sympathising side from you. It's because I wanna lay down my vulnerable side to you to let you know that you are important and not someone in general.

I know that all these things are very repetitive, coming from you but trust me, I can say these end a number of times literally because all these things come straight from my soul and not brain (which I really don't have). I really wished to write you an elongated letter for conveying all these things.

Just another special point which I'll like to mention, *I love writing letters but I have written for very specific and selective people in my life.* After all my blurry past, writing such an unfiltered letter, all over again, putting all my heart onto this piece of paper using my pen of emotions was of course difficult but just the thought of you reading it and giving different cute expressions made it easier and my heart knew how to describe its feelings for my homie right now.

You know what, I had never imagined this concept of what we are having previously. It was completely after meeting you and how the flow of things went which led us to our imperfect yet perfect sync. Isn't that something very beautiful and underrated too?

"If my happiness had a face, it would surely be you."

Cheers to you for making us come into existence!

I owe you a lot for this!

TWO
LETTER 2 : THE BURSTED BUBBLE...

Hardly had I scrawled towards the bed callously,
When those insane drops of blood dripped along my tiny finger,
I held the footboard of the bed aside to grab a streak of light ,
Peeping through the wooden window.
The light seemed contrary to the darkness which overpowered my soul right then,
I wondered how incapable I felt to feel anything else,
But you in everything around me,
The moonlight reflected on my fresh red blood- stained palm,
As the gleaming sparkle in your ocean- deep eyes.
I was confused either to burn in the fire of my heart,
Or freeze in the coldness of your eyes while I was casually getting side - zoned.
The night breeze tossed a knife to my scars of the fear,
Of losing you ever after not belonging to you.
The old rosewood tree stood intact,

Unattended to scream as my unheard cries during the night.

The folded bud started wilting away,

To crush the already broken expectations of my unrequited love,

The dew drops on the green carpet shone as bright as the beautiful pearls ,

Having trails of my anxiety hidden in them.

The full moon spread wholesome brightness all around,

Still that wasn't enough to extinguish the faded darkness in my soul.

A wave of indescribable rays fluttered across my heart,

All of a sudden, the flow of my thoughts changed.

Your brown eyes gave me an indispensable hope,

Every time I got drowned in them.

I got those eccentric shock running throughout my body,

When your glistened skin touched mine.

That could put even the most turbulent thunderstorm to shame.

Your deep breath got entangled in mine as our tongues embraced each other,

Only to weaken my already knocked knees.

Your firm embrace to my naked body through gentle hands sent a tingling sensation down through my spine.

Our legs were crossed with each other and our fingers were intertwined,

With our eyes gazing deep down our souls.

My heart was fluttering, with new sets of hope,

And another chance to feel the feeling of love again,

To love you by everything and to get loved by your everything.

The feeling was invincible enough to make me assured about giving all my love,

But wasn't invincible enough to receive all of it.

That was when another wave of breeze aroused the soothing pain,

As a drop of blood dripped against my fist,

The bubble of my seemingly last chance to feel love bursted apart.

THREE
LETTER 3 : NOT BETTER THAN YOUR EX FOR SURE...

I'm not better than your ex for sure,

but I'm definitely someone you will wish to hold your hand with while crossing the road.

I'm not better than your ex for sure,

but I'm definitely someone you will wish to stroke across your hair when you'll be tired,

I'm not better than your ex for sure,

but I'm definitely someone you will wish to pamper after a breakdown at midnight,

I'm not better than your ex for sure,

but I'm definitely someone you will wish to feed with your hands,

I'm not better than your ex for sure,

but I'm definitely someone you will wish to hold tightly during your much needed hug,

I'm not better than your ex for sure,

but I'm definitely someone you will wish to laugh with endlessly on logicless jokes,

I'm not better than your ex for sure,

but I'm definitely someone you will wish to cry with during a low night,

I'm not better than your ex for sure,

but I'm definitely someone you will wish to share things which you don't feel comfortable to do with others,

I'm not better than your ex for sure,

but I'm definitely someone worth remembering when I'm not around.

I'm definitely not better than your ex but I'm not the worst for sure.

FOUR

LETTER 4 : LOVE IS... ; LOVE ISN'T...

"Not everyone has their first love successful and so am I."

Although I have learnt that it's the failed relationships which actually lets you learn an abundance of lessons and learn what the actual meaning of love is in a far better manner when you actually get someone right.

Love isn't flawless.

It's accepting each other's flaws in the most genuine way to refine even better.

Love isn't worthless.

It's transforming a worthless person worthy of standing up for another person however worse the situation may seem.

Love isn't chaos less.

It's fighting for a million times and apologising the very next time to avoid the tears in the eyes of your special person.

Love is doubtless.

It's complaining to each other for petty reasons and still having an undoubtful trust in your heart.

Love is limitless.

It's making that one person feel the most special in numerous countless ways.

Love is bountifulness.

It's going to the maximum extent for that person's happiness in the most selfless way.

Love is clueless.

It's immersing yourself unconditionally for your true one without even realising the same.

Love is priceless.

It's securing a precious smile on that beautiful countenance which soothes your heart.

Love isn't the so-called dedication showcased nowadays but the selflessly genuine feeling for that one person sustained blooming better with each passing moment.

Love is imperfectly perfect; one of the rarest cherubic sanctions only a handful of lucky ones are truly blessed with!

Love isn't life certainly; but it's one of the most cherished feelings in the world with an unique invincibility to turn your life into a bit more beautiful one.

"Love is a bittersweet bliss!"

FIVE

LETTER 5 : TOGETHER AS BITTERSWEET HOMIES...

You are a ray of thunderstorm,
Striking across the sky and making my heart jump in ecstasy.
Although I'm in a deep chaos,
You are the sizzling breeze, echoing in my ears,
That pulls me to run and get drenched in extreme happiness.
Each time when you care for me,
Every time when you are there for me,
Each time you wipe my tears at midnight,
Every time you kiss me until I stop weeping,
Each hug of yours which melts all my chaps away,
Every time you try fading my dark times' ray,
I fell in love with you a bit more.

You love my flaws , accepting them so beautifully ,
You help me fight my insecurities in a stronger way,
You order midnight crunchies for my cravings,
You dance and get drenched with me during rain,
You are my bestest buddy I could have ever have,
You are my parallel shooting star in my universe,
You are the person to have the credit of my happiness
even though I believe that my happiness depends only on me.
We are so goofy together fella,
I get irritated easily and you love irritating me,
You listen more and I love speaking to you,
In the platter of matar paneer, you are the matar and I relish being the panneer ,
I go for clicking pics anywhere and you tend to photobomb them,
That's how we make two different pieces of a jigsaw puzzle fit together.
Your breathe near my ears feel so soothing,
Your touch to my skin feels so relaxing,
It takes me to the world of Utopia,
When you hold me from back to mesmerise my soul,
When you catch hold of my finger while crossing the road,
Even when you be angry every now and then,
You don't stop caring for me anytime,
I complain, I shout but above all I really adore and value you,
I don't know if eternity is real or not but let's just try on till whenever.

SIX

LETTER 6 : MY HOMIE HAS BEAUTIFUL EYES, NOSE, LIPS AND VIBES...

Your brown eyes are the most mesmerising pair I have ever encountered. Just a glance of the same can put me to an ultimate freezing phase. They reflect the words translated by the silence which is hidden in your heart. Your eyes are powerful enough to instantly calm the chaos which my soul encounters anytime.Those pretty eyelashes are a cherry on the cake to your magnificent brown pearls. Every pain of mine starts scattering just as sand from a fist as soon as my eyes get a glance of yours. Planting a kiss on your soulful eyes rejuvenates my heart and soothes my soul in an indescribable manner.

How can I overlook that cute nose of yours which seems perfect irrespective of its flaws? Moreover, it's the beautiful imperfections which give a flawless touch to your nose. That look you give while I squeeze your nose gently radiates angelic vibes. Rubbing my nose across yours transfers my soul to an altogether different paradise. Your ears seem like those of a rabbit. I know you won't agree but that is indeed true.

Have you ever noticed the soft petals of a fresh rose which blooms reflecting the silvery moonlight? Your lips outshine the softness of the same whenever you speak. The charm of your pinkish lips to me exists in the similar way as pink lotus petals are for bumblebees. Those lips of yours can hypnotise me with an intensity more than any magician could ever do. No tickling can make me feel the butterflies which I feel when your lips touch mine so carelessly.

Your ruffled hair keeps on dropping on your forehead callously to play hide and seek. They flutter as a mischievous crown on your head along the direction of the breeze. I feel at ease when I run my fingers through your silk strands. It provides me a bliss of another level when you put your head on my lap and sleep like a baby peacefully. Caressing your fragile hair locks while gazing at its texture whenever you sleep as such is something I would love doing for hours.

Your glowing face can melt even the coldest of hearts. Something of that kind has never crossed my way before. It's a vibe which is just replaceable and unique, just as the moon in the sky full of stars. At any state of my mind, whenever I see you laughing carelessly, happier than the happiest kid existing, I feel as if there are stars radiating bright amidst your smile.

"You are a **divine ray of hope** emerging in my life as the warm sun shining from the dark clouds.

You are the **moon** which calms me in the most chaotic situations as no one else can.

You are that **beautiful rose** blooming brightest in the garden of abundant flowers.

You are the **golden puff of a cigarette** which converts all worries to an invisible cloud of pacifying air.

You are the **fire shot of the liquor** which sensualizes the aura to a fantasy as soon as inhaled within.

You are the **first sip of morning tea** which soothes the heart as soon as the cup touches the lips."

SEVEN

LETTER 7 : THE BURNING PASSION IN MY HEART...

I'll make you my demigod to bow in front of you and worship you in praise.

I'll lay all my prayers to be with you and to rest my head on your shoulder for peace.

I'll promise a vow in your name by tying a thread.

I'll imprint the beauty of your heart on the paper of my life.

I'll turn all the rocks to make you an unbreakable habit of mine so that I can never distance myself from you.

Let me make you a burning passion in my heart.

I'll put you and only you to be a beautiful desire in my stars.

I'll cherish you as the deepest adoration of my soul.

Let me make you a burning passion in my heart.

Why do these boundaries and confinement exist which stops me from reaching close to you?

Why is this distance not decreasing between the two of us?

Why are our paths different even if we crave for the same destination?

Let me make you a burning passion in my heart.

I'll turn you into aesthetic pieces of my poetry and musings to let you know that you're the one for me.

I'll write your name on rocks so that it never gets erased just the way it's inscribed on my heart.

I'll make your voice into repetitive echoes which never stop screaming into my ears.

Let me make you a burning passion in my heart.

I'll turn you into the most beautiful adornment in my life.

I'll turn you into the reason for my smile even without uttering a single word.

I'll turn you into a precious blessing showered by the Almighty for me.

Let me make you a burning passion in my heart.

This vast ocean is the testimony of my love for you.

Is loving you such a punishable crime for me?

Is this limitless sky benevolent enough to tell you the limitless intensity I feel for you?

I'll even accept any punishment if my eyes get soothed by having a glance of yours.

Let me make you a burning passion in my heart...

...because love is nothing if I don't have a burning passion for you in my heart!

EIGHT

LETTER 8 : THE DREAMY FANTASY OF THAT LOVELY NIGHT AND US...

The sky full of stars was twinkling bright,
    You and I were enjoying the beautiful sight,
    The waves of the ocean kissed our feet,
    As we rested ourselves on the grainy golden blanket.
    The moon sprinkled all its silver dust across,
    Your face looked more adorable in the moonlight even
with flaws,
    With a glitter in your eyes as deep as the sea,
    And your ruffled hair flutters playfully with the breeze.
    Your dimpled cheeks were craving for attention,
    Till I pulled them as my special possession,
    Our bodies quivered when the winter gust blew,
    Contrary to our souls which felt all warm and fuzzy so
true.

I caressed your messy hair while rejoicing the serene weather,
With our fingers intertwined which brought us even closer,
I rested my head upon your built shoulder,
Which rendered me the solace of the whole world.
I squeezed your hands tighter in mine,
Just to feel the tranquillity of your presence so divine,
Our lips were quiet with no words exchanged,
And still our hearts felt the limitless love they contained.
The sky and the universe gleamed in glee,
I looked up to the shooting star for us as a plea,
In order to save our togetherness from being jinxed,
I stared at you continuously without any blinks.
The clouds were glowing to add to the beauty of the night sky,
I wondered why this beautiful moment kept on passing by,
I thanked the universe to have got you as a treasure,
Wishing to cherish you, us and this lovely night forever.

NINE

LETTER 9: THE SHADOW OF BRIGHT LIGHT...

Even the thing with all virtues would have one or another vice and the same would go for love too.

> "*No two individuals can have their opinions carbon copied and that's the basic reason for our conflicts too.*"

We do fight, we yell and we scream. Sometimes it's me whose yells are louder, sometimes it's you and sometimes it's our tantrums which control our moods. Fighting with each other becomes the situation instantly but the motive should be always fighting with the clashed opinion in a combined manner to sort the same. That's the same which I would prefer to do with you anyday and always.I know my anger issues are something which I really need to work upon but trust me, my trials are on.

I am trying to control my irrational anger and tantrums which I show you. I wish those efforts work on but I really want to thank you for bearing with me. Even the waves of the ocean try to clash with one another as they have different ranges of splash, although they merge in consequently. Similarly, even after having quarrels, I would choose sorting to the earliest in order to choose you because it's you which I want at the end of the day however.

I had heard that people start questioning themselves during quarrels and it's true to some extent. Even I get questions if this whole thing is worth the chaos, fights, etc. or not during times when we are on rough terms. For instance, it really has the power to confuse your soul in a damned way. However, in those times too, all that matters is my trust on my decisions, you and me. It provides an invisible power to me in a jiffy after all quarrels in a way to strengthen our bond in an even better way.

Your breath merging in mine is the best amalgamation I could experience,
The sight of my emotions reflecting in your gleaming eyes makes me feel a complete universe,
Your presence in my arms tickles the butterflies in my stomach like a teenage love,
Let's feel the best for receiving this fairy tale.
The snow around got melted by the warmth of our togetherness,
Our laughter echoed in the whole valley with ear to ear wide smiles,
Our crazy friendship merged with abundance of love, tagged us goofy buddies,
The whole universe was visible to them in each other's ocean deep eyes,

A new venture together, a new adventure and a new lovely phase along with flaws and insecurities,
Blessed by the divine aura to be intertwined till eternity.

TEN

LETTER 10 :BINDING MY OVERTHINKING SOUL WITH YOUR DOSE OF LOVE...

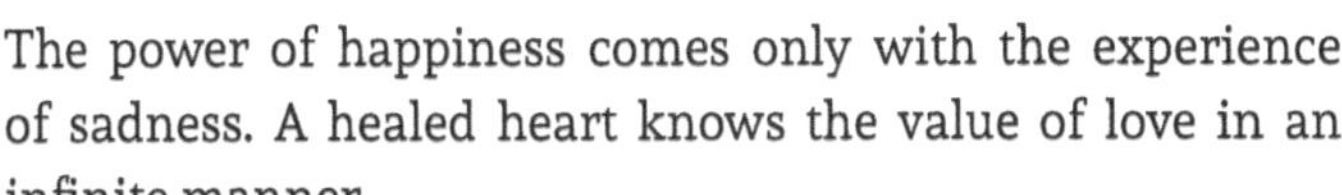

The power of happiness comes only with the experience of sadness. A healed heart knows the value of love in an infinite manner.

There are lots of insecurities, jealousy, fear of being replaced, fear of not being enough, etc. and this is because I wish us to be better for each other with the maximum happiness. That is the only reason for all these negative ideas and over-thinking to erupt inside me. Although the way you hold me and calm my heart irrespective of how low I feel is what my soul craves for everytime when something goes wrong.

Having the thought of you being present in my life is enough for me to bring a cherubic smile on my countenance. The best thing is that my existence stays sound even after being with you. I can be my real self and yet there is a wholesome acceptance between the two of us. I know you aren't a huge fan of words as I am but your eyes speak everything for me and maybe that's enough for my soul. Your actions show the paramount concern you encase for me from the point you put on hand on the corner of the kitchen slab in order to avoid me getting hurt to letting me walk on the safer side of the road. The way you calm me down on my random breakdowns is something which even I wouldn't be able to do in such a manner.

"The bright twilight is dimmer than the happiness which I naturally get when you are around. Each and every star of the universe has planned to bring us together on the same terms and I believe we are lucky to have each other's back ♥."

Let The Stars Decide...

People say forever is an illusion and maybe it's so.

The perfect vibe about our bond as two imperfect people is that we both don't give a damn about tomorrow. It's today where we live, enjoying moments with each other being in it, cherishing the memories made, and being grateful for the happy times we are having together. The expectations of staying together with each other isn't present till the farthest point which increases the peace and happiness we feel manifold. I adore you having this immense faith in this ideology of staying in the present. Basically, it's just the present which we can control and handle accordingly. That way, all the enjoyable moments are felt at its best and nothing is missed out.

The expectations are kept in check which eventually increases the happiness level of both of us and moulds our bond in a lovelier manner altogether. Keeping hopes above everything, I can't describe the level of the gratitude I have for you to accept my imperfect existence in a perfect manner.

Just a thought of yours and each and everything seems to be moving towards the best. I wonder how a person can be a perfect replication of what Utopia can make you feel like.

"Forever isn't forever, so, let's vibe till whenever."